Manufactured in the United States

Any resemblance to actual events or persons, living or dead, is entirely coincidental. This is in no form meant for harm nor do we promote harm. Personal perspective use only. Please do not copy/mimic any words or illustration from this book.

Illustrations by Cameron Wilson for Soulsimplicity Design and Publishing.
for illustration inquires visit camdaillastrata.com.

Malik, Olivia, & Antonio's Lake Park Adventure

By Sherefa T. Green

Illustrated by Cameron Wilson

DEDICATION

This book is dedicated to Antonio, Olivia, and Malik Smith. This is a Children's book that is constructed around everyday discussion that will help children cope, cultivate, and empower them to deal with everyday life. It will motivate them to bring out the Kings and the Queens in their personalities. This book also introduces Biblical principles at every discussion to help their minds become more fertile; which in return they will find peace, joy, and strength; without too much micromanagement. Moreover, it would lead to different outcomes as they go through life's challenges and experiences to refresh, reinstate, and renew, that will later produce a profitable future. Kingdom Legacies

CONTENTS

	Acknowledgments	i
1	Chapter One	1-2
2	Chapter Two	3-5
3	Chapter Three	6-9
4	Chapter Four	10-12
5	Chapter Five	13-16
6	Chapter Six	17-19
7	Chapter Seven	20-23
8	Chapter Eight	24-28

ACKNOWLEDGMENTS

First and foremost, I would like to thank my Heavenly Father (Abba). Without Him this Vision would not be possible. Secondly, I would like to thank my gorgeous Suga Dumpling my mother Marcia Palmer for her love and support. She believed in me every step of the way. I am so grateful thanks.

To Next Level Faith Center under the dynamic Leadership of Apostle Lashon Reese and Pastor Olden Reese. My Beautiful god parents. I love y'all so much, words could never express my gratitude. To Warriors on the Wall Prayer group (W.O.W) under their Powerful Leadership of Prophetess Tracy Magwood, it is because of the prayers and the grace of God that I made it this far and beyond. Last, but not least to Michelle Watson for her diligence, and heartfelt help. And everyone that contributed to make this Vision possible, I appreciate it all, thank you so much. Yahweh, Yahweh. Blessings!

CHAPTER ONE

Everyday around 12 noon Malik would get up, brush his teeth, dry his face and rush to his mom's room overwhelmingly excited, because today is the day that he knew that his mom would take him to the park. He slightly opened his mom's room door, climbed on the side of her bed, leaned over to kiss her sleepy face as he gently pressed his little fingers on her cheeks and rubbed his cold hands up against her warm skin.

"Mom! Get up! Mom, Mom!" Malik repeated. "Are you up? It's time to go to the park. Mom! Get up! Did you hear me?"

With his warm kiss, soft touch, and gentle voice, mom began to awaken from her sleep.

"Yes Malik. What do you want?" Mom asked sleepily.

"Remember you said you'll take us to the park," said Malik.

"Yes," Mom replied.

"Well, me, Antonio, and Olivia are ready," said Malik.

Mom groaned tiredly and thrust the blue blanket back over her head.

"Mom, please get up!" anxiously said Malik. "I'll buy you something."

"Like what Malik?" asked Mom.

"Jewelry," said Malik.

Since Mom likes to keep her promises most of the time, she tilted her head back and forth, turned on her side, sat up, and placed her feet on the ground. She then slides her beautiful red polished toes into the beautiful red fluffy slippers awaiting at the side of her bed.

Malik ran out of mom's room. "Antonio! Olivia! Wake up, wake up, wake up! It's time to go!"
"Malik, what do you want?" They both softly whisper.

"Mom is getting dressed to take us to the park," said Malik.

"We going to the park!" screamed Olivia, as she wasted no time jumping out of her bed. She headed to her closet, changed her sleeping wear to a more appealing attire.

CHAPTER TWO

"Ayeee we are going to the park; we are going to the park!" Malik sang. "Antonio are you dressed?"

"No Malik! I can't find my shirt!" yelled Antonio.

"You can never find your shirt Bonio Tonio," teased Malik.

"Leave me alone and go watch tv. I can't concentrate," said Antonio.

"Olivia!" Antonio called out.

"Yes," she answered as she rushed from the living room with a half-eaten cookie in her hand.

"Have you seen my shirt?" asked Antonio.

"No," she answered with a mouth stuffed full of cookies.

"I know you saw it, cause all your clothes are on my side of the closet," said Antonio.

"How I'm supposed to see your shirt Antonio, when I don't even know which shirt you're looking for?" asked Olivia.

"Never mind Olivia you make no sense!" Antonio yelled.

"How I make no sense, when you're the one asking me for a shirt you can't find, and I don't even know what color you're looking for?" Olivia quickly yells back.

As the two begin to go back and forth at each other Malik went on top of Olivia's bunk bed to retrieve his toys. While coming down from the top bunk Malik threw down a white T-shirt that was hanging on the side of the railing.

"Here you go Antonio Bonio," said Malik.

"Please stop saying that. It's not funny Malik, you're always trying to rhyme my name," said Antonio annoyed.

"Ok Tonio Bonio," teased Malik.

Olivia laughed as cookies fell out of her mouth.

"Ma!" yelled Antonio, "Can you get Malik?"

"Malik!" called Mom

"Yes!" answered Malik.

"Come here!" yelled Mom.

"I'm coming," answered Malik. Malik turns and whispers to Antonio. "Bye Antonio Bonio."

"Ma!" yelled Antonio, "He's doing it again!"

"No, I'm not," Malik said pitifully as he ran out the bedroom.

CHAPTER THREE

Mom was in the kitchen warming up some hot water on the stove to make some coffee. She heard a sweet little voice whisper, "Can I have some chocolate milk please?"

As the energetic 3-year-old Malik, batted his deep, memorizing brown eyes, Mom turned and asked him "Aren't you tired of drinking chocolate milk?"

"No!" Malik said frantically.

"Why do you like chocolate milk anyway?" asked Mom.

With a smart remark, Malik answered his mother back, "Cause, since you told me I can't have coffee, chocolate milk looks like it Ma."

Mom looked up to the ceiling gracefully and said "Lord help me! This is my fault; I drank too much Frappe with him when I was pregnant."

"I want it hot please Mom," he said as he ran yelling towards the living room.

Meanwhile, everyone was getting dressed, and Grandma was in the bathroom getting dolled up. When she opened the door, we all smiled and said "OHHH! THAT'S PRETTY!"

"O' Grandma!" Olivia said. "I love your light green linen shirt, with your blue jeans, and black boots, with your pearl necklace!"

Malik asked, "Where are you going Grandma?"

Grandma blushed as she starts to strut her runway walk in the hallway, elegantly lighting up the room. "Thanks, I'm blessed," She said as she blew an air kiss in the mirror.

"Awww honey honey grandma's my favorite girl," Malik sang.

"Is everyone ready?!" yelled Mom.

"I'm ready," said Malik.

"I knew you would be ready baby," replied Mom.

"Where's my warm chocolate milk Ma?" asked the 3-year-old.

"Right here bae," said Mom.

"I can't find my shoes," Antonio said.

Grandma upsettingly tells Antonio, "You move too slow. You can never find your stuff, but you can always find everybody else's. If we are not careful, you'll make us late for everything."

After a few tosses around in the shoe closet, Antonio finally finds his shoes.

"Ok. I-10 by 10," said Mom. "Let's move it!"

She slowly opens the front door, while the children rush towards her excitedly running down the stairs. They then realized that Grandma was missing.

"Where is Grandma?" Mom asked.

"She's up the stairs," Olivia said.

"Wait mom! Wait! We can't leave Grandma!" said Malik.

Shortly after, Grandma yelled, "Do y'all have your masks?"

"No," replied the children. "We left it on the couch."

"Well, I can't remember everything for y'all," said Grandma.

"O' Grandma," said Olivia. "We're sorry. Can you bring it for us, my beautiful Queen?"

"Ask your Mom does she have her mask," said Grandma.

"Mom!" Olivia yelled. "Grandma said do you have your mask?"

"Yes, I do, it's in my bag," replied Mom.

The children were playing around for a few minutes on the sidewalk before Grandma came downstairs. Across the sidewalk shined a gorgeous ray of light. Mom quickly gathered the children together and took a group picture.

"O' here comes Grandma," the children said.

"Say cheese Grandma, take a picture," Malik insisted.

"Mom," the children's mother asked, "Where are you going with all those bags? We are just going to the park suga dumpling."

"Yea, but I need all these supplies just in case my grandchildren get thirsty or bit," said Grandma.

"O', okay. You have a valid point," Mom responded back.

CHAPTER FOUR

"STOP!" yelled Mom, as the children started to run towards the car. "WAIT! Look both ways before you cross the street! Just wait I'm coming!"

(Click Click)

The car door opened. Antonio rushed over to open the door for his mother. "I got it Mom, excuse me Olivia. I need to open the car door for Mom. Olivia!" Antonio said, "I'm a boy I have to open the door."

"I wanted to open the door too!" said Olivia upsettingly. She went to the other side and tried to open the passenger side for grandma.

"Olivia!" Antonio said. "I said I'll open up the doors."

"That's not fair," said Olivia.

Mom interrupted the conversation. "Olivia it's okay he's a boy, if he said he wants to open up the car door let him." Unhappily, Olivia stormed into the car.

"Fix your attitude little girl or nobody will be going to the park." Mom said sternly.

"Olivia!" Malik said, "Come on be good."

The car automatically started, and the Bluetooth connected to mom's phone.

"Is that Pastor Matthew?' asked Malik.

"YES!" Mom replied. "Now everyone be quiet. I can't hear." Mom noticed through her rear-view mirror that Malik and Olivia looked at each other and started smiling. Not long after mom was on the highway, Malik yelled, "FASTER MOM FASTER!"

"This is not a race Malik." Said Mom.

"Then why are you driving so fast?" asked Malik.

"Because she's on the highway," said Olivia.

Grandma started saying a prayer in her head as always, as mom excelled the highway. Malik started to annoy mom by tapping on the back of her seat. "Are we there yet mom?" he asked.

"No!" Mom yelled.

"Well roll down my window please Mom?" asked Malik.

"She can't roll down the window," said Olivia.

"Certainly, Mom can roll down the window Olivia, because she's not driving too fast anymore," said Malik.

Out of the blue Antonio said, "Mom I remember the scripture."

"What scripture?" asked Mom.

"Psalm 1. Do you want to hear it?" asked Antonio.

"Yes, go ahead." Said Mom.

"Psalm 1… Blessed is the man that walketh not in the counsel of the ungodly, not stand in the way of sinners north sentinel seat of the scornful what is the lightest in the law of the Lord and in his love and best he meditate day and night he shall be like a tree planted by the rivers of water that bringeth forth fruit in his season. His leaf shall not wear them whatsoever he doeth shall prosper young girl you're not so but are like the chest that the wind river the way there for the ungodly shall not stand in the judgment, nor sinners in the congregation of the righteous. for the Lord knows the way of the righteous but the way of the ungodly shall perish." recited Antonio.

"Okay, okay I see you remember the scriptures! Congratulations!" said Mom, almost missing the turn. "We're here."

"Yes, thank God!" said Malik eagerly taking off his seat belt.

"Stop! Wait until I stop driving and park," said Mom.

"But you said we're here," said Malik.

"Yes, I know what I said. Just relax bae! Let me Park." said Mom.

CHAPTER FIVE

Everyone began to climb out the car. Malik un-hooked his seat belt and started to crawl to the front of the car.

"I was coming to get you, I wasn't going to leave you in the car," said Mom.

"O' Look this is pretty. It's nice and green," said Olivia.

"Look Ma look!" the children screamed. "The other kids are riding their bicycles, and there's a statue of a man over there sitting down with a little girl with her legs crossed."

"Antonio look, look, look!" Olivia yelled while jumping up and down. "It's a lake, it's a big silver lake!"

Antonio said, "It's not a silver lake Olivia, it's just a lake."

Left foot, right foot, as we climb up the hill, then down onto the track pavement.

"Excuse me," a humble voice said as he rode his bike over the lake bridge. We begin to see a lot of children and elderly people holding hands. People from all walks of life, different colors, races, ages, and backgrounds. As we all began to explore the park the view was amazing. Children were fishing with their dads. This one little girl had on all pink, sitting in her pink seat, with her pink hat, with her pink fishing rod, and pink buck.

"Uncle David! Uncle David!" yelled the children altogether.

"Where?" Mom said, "Oh wow, I forgot he was even here with us for a second because he was so quiet."

"Look!" screamed Olivia, while she jumped up and down with a big smile on her face, "Want to go fishing?"

"We don't have any fishing supplies," said Uncle David, "Maybe next time."

David started to lean his head over to look into the lake, while Antonio and Grandma were reading the park signs.

"Uncle David," said Malik, "What are you looking for?"

"I'm looking for frogs," replied Uncle David.

"Frogs in the lake? They might be frozen." said Malik.

Uncle David began to laugh. "Frozen! You're funny Malik."

"Guys! Hurry! Hurry!" Olivia and Antonio happily screamed, as they were running across the old wooden but steady bridge. Incredibly, they were well behaved.

Mom was recording everyone as they walked, and suddenly Antonio ran towards her and said "Mom, can you tackle me like we are playing Football?"

"Tackle you?" Mom said. Unknowingly, he had no idea that mom use to play a little football back in her days. This was going to be an easy treat for her.

"If you want me to tackle you, someone has to record," said Mom.

"Grandma, can you hold the camera so Mom can tackle me?" asked Antonio.

"I want to be free today," said Grandma.

"Come on!" said Antonio. "Fine! I'll ask Olivia." "Olivia! Come here!" Antonio called out. "Can you record me while Mom tackles me?"

"Ok this is going to be fun!" she laughed.

Olivia was holding the camera unsteadily as she began to jump up and down with excitement, running with the camera, repeating Mom tackling Antonio.

Antonio tried to block his mother. She went to the left, and she went to the right. Then she grabbed him and held him upside down letting him go slowly as she took off running speedily. She realized, he wasn't able to catch up with her, so she stopped for a second. She repeats the first action as she did before, not shortly after, Antonio breathing heavily with a scratch on his arm said, "I'm hurt a little, but I'm not crying."

Malik rushed over to his Mom like he's captain save a lot; and said, "What did you do that for Mom?" as he grabbed onto her legs defending his bigger brother.

"We just playing," she told him, "Relax bae."

Once again, Antonio started to run, this time he broke free within seconds as Mom began to run. Mom's foot slid on the gravel and she almost fell, but she caught her balance right at the end. "That's enough," she said, "that's enough. We're close to the other side of the lake anyways."

"Everybody, stop! Grab an adult's hand. This bridge does not have any guard rails." said Mom.

CHAPTER SIX

"Oh wow!" said Mom and David.

"Look there's a house over on top of the hill. Did y'all go over there?" asked David.

"NO! Hopefully, we can go over there," said Grandma. "Stop guys! This bridge has no railing. Everybody just take your time and relax."

We set out onto the bridge that made the pathway through the middle of the lake, as we began to walk towards the center of the mini rest house that was setup.

"I need to drink my coffee. I'm putting you down. I'm tired," Mom said to Malik.

"I'm tired too," Malik replied.

"How are you tired when I'm the one that's carrying you?" asked Mom.

"I don't know ma, but I'm just tired. Drink your coffee," replied Malik.

"I can't Malik. I can't. It's hot, and you're in my hands. This is ridiculous," complained Mom. "You are too old for this."

"Mom, it's hot and my feet hurt. I can't help it, I'm ridiculously little," Malik said, as he looked at his Mom and smiled.

"Really!" said Mom.

"Mom, you're the one with the powers so make it go away," said Malik.

"That's it boy I'm putting you down. I don't have any powers. You the one with the powers," said Mom.

Just as Mom was getting ready to put Malik down, a fair light skinned lady with light blonde hair, and two handsome boys with blue eyes said, "Here you go."

Mom looked over as she handed her a bag full of bread.

"Would you like to feed the ducks?" she asked.

"Yes!" the children said excitedly.

Since mom's hands were occupied with Malik, her coffee, and the camera, Uncle David took the bag of bread from her. The fair lady began to explain that her boys doesn't eat the back of the bread, and that there were leftover half eaten peanut butter and jelly sandwiches left in the bag.

Mom laughed. She found it strange that they ate peanut butter and jelly sandwiches. She replied, "Me neither. I also don't like the back of the bread."

"MOM! The ducks! Put me down!" exclaimed Malik.

"Boy! You ain't gotta tell me twice!" said Mom. "Look! There's ducks, and swans!"

"NO! It's ducks, and geese," said the fair lady's husband.

"O," said Mom, and Uncle David.

Uncle David took a whole bread out of the bag, broke it into pieces, and threw it in the water. The ducks, and geese started swimming close to eat the soggy bread.

"Let me try," said Olivia. Uncle David gave her a whole bread, and she threw all of it into the water.

Malik said, "I want to try too," and he also threw the whole bread into the unfiltered water.

"NO!" Uncle David said, "You have to break the bread into bite size, piece by piece, or y'all are going to run out of bread fast."

"Sherefa, David! Look there are a whole lot more ducks and baby ducklings on this side," yelled Grandma.

Olivia got up and started running.

"Careful," Grandma said, as Malik ran behind her.

Mom handed the camera off to Grandma and kneeled on her knees to help her children feed the ducks. Malik laid across her back, and all of a sudden, a cool wind blew, and time stood still!

CHAPTER SEVEN

"WOAH! MOM, MOM! Look," said Malik.

"Unfortunately, Mom can't hear you, or see me young prince." a beautiful Angelic voice said. She had long eyelashes, feathers as white as snow, with black lining around her neck, a smooth black beak to match, and was the size of a middle-sized yacht.

"Who said that?" asked Antonio.

"I don't know," said Olivia.

"Look guys the swan is speaking," said Malik.

"They can't see me young prince," said the magical Goose.

"Well, how come I can see you and they can't?" asked Malik, "I must have fed you too many peanut butter and jelly sandwiches."

"Ha, ha, ha," the Goose laughed gracefully.

"Well, since you must know. When you were laying across your Mom's back you wished that I were real," explained the Goose, "You did it with the power of your mind."

"I did?" asked Malik.

"Yes, you did my young prince, and that's why I am here," said the Goose. "Maybe if you try wishing for your brother and sister to see me, they just might."

Malik began to wish in his mind that Olivia, and Antonio could see the Magical Goose. A cool breeze blew, and all of a sudden, their eyes were opened too.

"MOM! UNCLE DAVID! GRANDMA!" cried out Antonio as he turned around walking backwards and losing his balance at the sight of the magical goose, transforming into a beautiful boat ride. Inside was gold, blue, purple, and green trimmers with a red staircase. She disappeared on the other side and caught Antonio right before he would ever touch the water.

"MOM!" cried Antonio, "Help me!"

"She can't hear you fair prince," said the Goose. "Only young prince, princess, and you can see or hear me."

"WOW!" exclaimed Olivia excitedly jumping up and down. "How did you do that?"

"It's simple by the power of your mind," said the Goose, "Just like young prince here brought me to life."

"My name is Malik," said Malik.

"Ok Prince Malik," said the Canadian Goose.

"I'm not a prince," responded Malik.

"Fine. I'll call you young king," replied the Goose.

"My Mom calls me that," said Malik.

"Then, young king it is," said the Goose.

"What's your name?" asked Olivia.

"Well princess my name is Lady Candice.," said the Goose.

"Lady Candice," said Olivia.

"Yes," she replied.

"What are you? And where did you come from?" asked Olivia.

"Well, princess, that's two good questions. I am a Canadian Goose. My family is originally from Canada. I was brought here when I was a little baby, just like your size on a big ship with a few of my family. I don't remember much, but from what I was told my mom chose this great lake to live on, with me, a few of my siblings, and my stepdad. And by the looks of it she did an AMAZING JOB. I can hear the pure hearts of children, just like I can hear young kings here; and transform their imaginations into life," explained Lady Candice.

"Wait! But why me Lady Goose?" Malik asked.

"It's Lady Candice, but you can call me Lady if you like," said Lady Candice. "Well, young king your heart is as pure as gold. It is a treasure that was found."

"Hello! I don't care what treasure was found. I want my mommy!" cried out Antonio. "Get me out of here!"

"The only way you can get out of here fair prince is by using the power of your mind," said Lady Candice.

(A song started to play)
'When you are thinking with the powers of your mind,
and you think your creation won't come out right,
dig a little deeper cause nothing is more powerful than the creation of your mind'

Then, out of nowhere a golden basket full of ice cream appeared in the boat ride.

"Wow! Olivia, do that again," said Malik.

"I want cake, candy, water, a new doll, and a princess outfit with a golden crown," wished Olivia.

CHAPTER EIGHT

"Would you two like to join, fair prince in the back of the ride?" asked Lady Candice.

"NO! Nobody joining nothing! We are all going to stay right where we are. I'm going to get out of this boat, and go back to our regular life," said Antonio.

"Ha, ha, ha," laughed Lady Candice, "Regular life fair prince, there is nothing regular anymore, and either are you."

"What do you mean?" asked Antonio.

"Well, for one you're talking to me, two you're in my back that's now a boat ride, and three young king, has accessed the power of his mind," explained Lady Candice.

"Okay, and what does that have to do with me?" Antonio asked frustrated. "You know what, you must be scornful."

"Move over boy," said Olivia as she climbed the stairs to get inside the Magical Goose ride.

"Yeah, Tonio Bonio move over with your scary self," teased Malik.

"Are you guys serious?" shouted Antonio. "What did mom say about speaking to strangers and taking rides from strangers."

Together Malik and Olivia said, "Stranger danger."

Olivia began to say, "Boy she's not a stranger. She's a duck. A magical duck that Malik brought to life with his mind. If you ask me boy, she looks perfectly fine to me."

"Ha, ha, ha!" laughed Lady Candice. "NO! He's right princess. Even though young king did bring me to life with his mind, fair prince is right. I'm still a stranger."

"Stranger danger, duck struck… whatever Lady Candice, is it was just my luck," said Malik.

"Ha, ha, ha!" Olivia laughed.

"Malik, this is not no time to laugh and rhyme, wish us back to normal," said Antonio.

"Move Tonio, Bonio welcome to my imagination," said Malik.

"Lady Candice," said Malik, "Lets ride!"

Antonio looked up at the sky and began to pray. This time he got it right. "Blessed is the man that walks not in the counsel of the ungodly. Nor standeth in the ways of sinners, nor sitteth in the seat of the scornful but his delight is in the law of the Lord; and in his law he meditates day and night. And he shall be like a tree planted by the rivers of water that bringeth fruit in his season; his leaf also shall not wither, and whatsoever he doeth shall prosper."

Little did Antonio know as he was repeating the prayer to himself the lake was transforming into every word he said. The water turned crystal blue with a steady flow. The heavens opened up over their heads with a phenomenal light leading the way. There were beautiful trees with unusual colors planted by the lake banks of all shapes and sizes.

"Your activation is my command," said Lady Candice silently to herself as Antonio began to use the power of his mind and words unknowingly.

"OMG!" said Olivia, "Malik what did you think about? It's beautiful! Boy you're good."

"That's not me Olivia, I thought that was you," said Malik.

"No! That is not me. I would ask for ice cream as we ride on," said Olivia. The more she thought the more things appeared.

"Olivia, leave room for me too," said Malik, "If you keep thinking there will not be enough room for Lady Goose." Lady Candice looked back at Malik, he laughed out loud, and said "I mean Lady Candice to carry."

"Ok young prince, I mean young king, there is no limit to my capacity," said Lady Candice.

Antonio finally took his head out the clouds and started to look around. "OMG where did all these things come from? Olivia you look beautiful," said Antonio amazed.

"Thank you," she replied.

"Wait, the lake looks different. It's AMAZING. What happened?" Antonio asked.

"We don't know," said Malik and Olivia.

"All I wished for," said Olivia, "is what's inside the boat. Everything else happened when you were back there praying as Lady Candice drove."

“Wait, are you serious?” asked Antonio.

“Yes, Bonio,” said Malik.

“NO! It can't be!” Antonio thought to himself.

“What?” said Olivia.

“You are so nosey if you must know. I was saying Psalm 1. Do you think I activated the power of mind out of beautiful fear? No, I couldn’t have,” said Antonio.

To make sure that he wasn’t losing his mind, Antonio began to think… let it rain green apples. Within seconds, it started raining green apples. Automatically, Olivia and Malik yelled at Antonio.

“What?” he said.

“We know that's you! Green apples! Boy, we are getting hit! Make it stop!” said Olivia. She wished for a shield, and a shield appeared around Lady Candice.

“Antonio,” said Malik, “We said stop it! We are in the water Bonio. How is Lady Candice going to swim?”

“You right Malik,” said Antonio. Within seconds it stopped raining green apples.

“I did it,” said Antonio.

“Yes, you did,” said Lady Candice.

"Wait, you can hear my inner thoughts too?" asked Antonio.

"Yes, fair prince. Job well done." Said Lady Candice.

Smiling proudly to himself, Antonio grabbed a green apple from the golden basket, leaned over on the side of Lady Candice, and bumped his forehead into his own forcefield.

"Oooosh!" he said, as he imagined the shield to be removed so he can enjoy the scenery.

Lady Candice gracefully smiled, bowing her head up and down as she drove at a faster pace onto the glistening lake.

Sherefa Tene Green was born November 9, 1988 in Kingston, Jamaica to the mother of Marcia Palmer and father Eyton Green. Being the only girl out of 5 boys she had to find her own beat, in her own lane. By the age of 8 her and her brother David L. Green was uprooted from their hometown and relocated to Miami, FL in 1996. During this time, she went to various schools. In 2006, she graduated cum laude From Miami Edison Sr. High. She also attended Florida Memorial University & Miami Dade College where she studied Biology, and a few other technical schools. She always had a dream of becoming an Orthopedic Surgeon or Pediatrician. "Sherefa loves the kids". She's Currently enrolled in Oakton College to further her studies. By the age of 23 she was married; during that period of her life, she gave birth to 3 beautiful angels Antonio, Olivia, and Malik Smith. However, life has its different mode of transportations. She currently resides in Evanston, Illinois where she finally created her metaphors of change, and love for writing during the COVID-19 Pandemic lockdown. This beautiful 32-year-old is uniquely talented and gifted. This Queen has finally taken her rightful place and reclaiming her rights in history. To the future, Kingdom Legacies.

9 798330 327935